Sleeping Beauty

Adapted by Thea Feldman
Illustrated by the Disney Storybook Art Team

 A GOLDEN BOOK • NEW YORK

randomhouse.com/kids
ISBN 978-0-7364-3233-7
Printed in the United States of America
10 9 8 7 6 5 4 3 2 1

Long ago, in a faraway land, King Stefan and his queen had a baby girl named Aurora. A great holiday was proclaimed throughout the kingdom. Everyone was invited to the castle to celebrate the arrival of the new princess.

Jolly King Hubert and his son Phillip came from a
neighboring kingdom to congratulate the new parents. Wishing
to unite their kingdoms, the two kings decided that Phillip and
Aurora would marry one day.

The three good fairies—Flora, Fauna, and Merryweather—
arrived with special gifts for Princess Aurora. Flora presented
the baby with the gift of beauty. Fauna gave the tiny princess
the gift of song.

Suddenly, the evil fairy Maleficent appeared in a blast of
fire and smoke. She was angry that she hadn't been invited.
She sneered at the crowd and declared, "Before the sun sets
on her sixteenth birthday, she shall prick her finger on the
spindle of a spinning wheel and die!"

The castle guards rushed to capture Maleficent, but she
vanished in a flash of lightning.

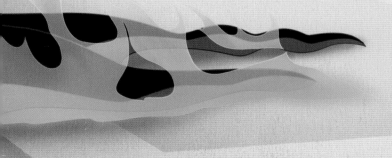

Luckily, Merryweather still had a magical gift to give the princess. The good fairy couldn't undo Maleficent's curse, but she was able to change it. Aurora would now fall into a deep sleep if she pricked her finger. As a vision of the sixteen-year-old princess materialized, the good fairy promised, "You shall wake when True Love's Kiss the spell shall break."

Fearful for his daughter's life, King Stefan had every spinning wheel in the kingdom destroyed. Flora came up with yet another plan to protect the princess. The good fairies would disguise themselves as peasant women and raise Aurora deep in the forest. They would do everything without magic, so Maleficent wouldn't suspect a thing.

King Stefan and the Queen knew Flora's plan was for the best. They watched with heavy hearts as their only child disappeared into the night with the three good fairies.

Sixteen years passed. Maleficent was frustrated that her henchmen had never located the princess. She turned to her pet raven and said, "You are my last hope. Circle far and wide. Search for a maid of sixteen with hair of sunshine gold and lips red as a rose."

In the forest, a happy girl named Briar Rose greeted the day from her cottage window. She did not know she was really the princess Aurora and that her "aunties" were the good fairies.

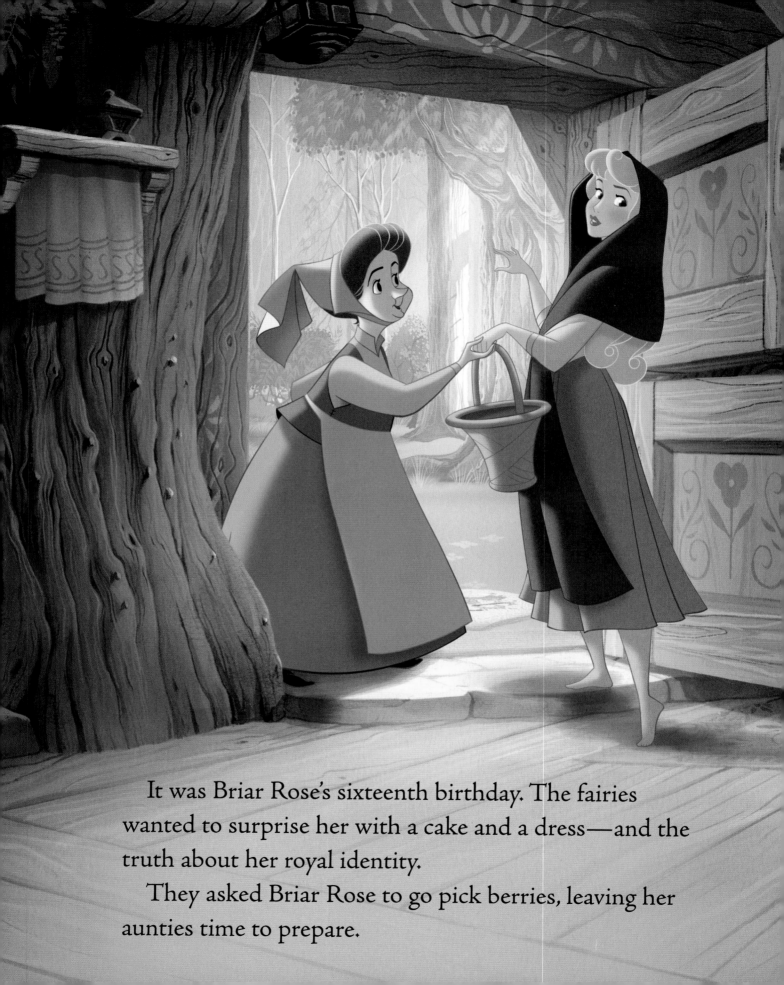

It was Briar Rose's sixteenth birthday. The fairies
wanted to surprise her with a cake and a dress—and the
truth about her royal identity.

They asked Briar Rose to go pick berries, leaving her
aunties time to prepare.

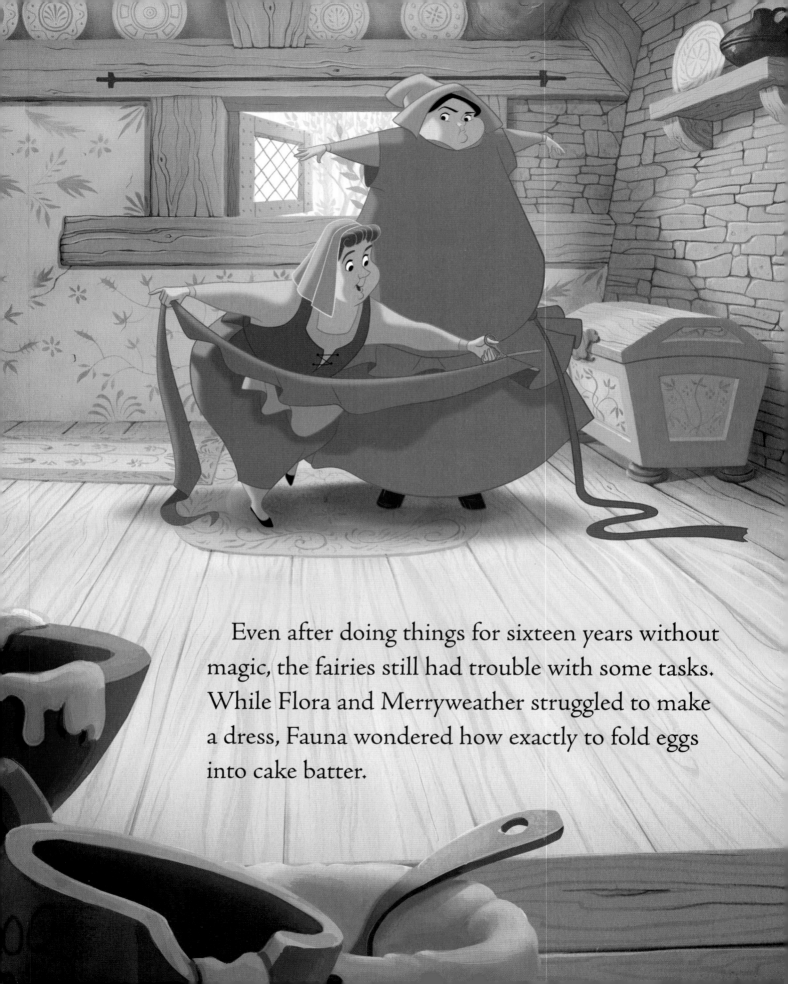

Even after doing things for sixteen years without magic, the fairies still had trouble with some tasks. While Flora and Merryweather struggled to make a dress, Fauna wondered how exactly to fold eggs into cake batter.

At the same time, Briar Rose happily visited with
her animal friends. She told them that she had met a
handsome prince . . . but only in her dreams. "They say
if you dream a thing more than once, it's sure to come
true," she sighed as she began singing and dancing.

There actually was a prince nearby! Prince Phillip spotted the beautiful girl and stepped out of the bushes to join her in a dance. They both felt as if they were in a dream.

Briar Rose invited the young man to see her again that evening at the cottage. Neither knew the other's name, only that they had fallen instantly—and deeply—in love.

Back at the cottage, Merryweather insisted that the
fairies give up on sewing and baking and instead use their
magic to make everything perfect for Briar Rose. With the
wave of a wand, a dress was created in an instant. But Flora
wanted it to be pink, while Merryweather wanted it to be
blue. As the fairies argued, they kept changing the dress's
color by sending magical sparks back and forth.

The colorful sparks soared up and out of the chimney as Maleficent's pet raven flew by. He stopped and saw Briar Rose return to the cottage. Then the wicked bird listened to all that was said before returning to Maleficent with a full report.

Briar Rose loved the dress and the cake, but she
couldn't wait to tell her aunties about the wonderful
young man she had just met. The fairies were shocked
and hurried to tell the girl her true identity—and that it
had already been arranged that she would marry a prince.

Many a young girl would delight at finding out she was a princess betrothed to a prince. But as Aurora dutifully accompanied the fairies to the castle, her only thoughts were of the young man she had just met— and already fallen in love with.

Before the sun set, the fairies
sneaked Aurora into the castle.
They presented her with her
crown and gave her a few minutes
alone. Aurora cried. She was
heartbroken knowing that fate
separated her from her true love.

Suddenly, a glowing green orb
appeared and put Aurora into a
trance. She followed the orb up
a winding staircase.

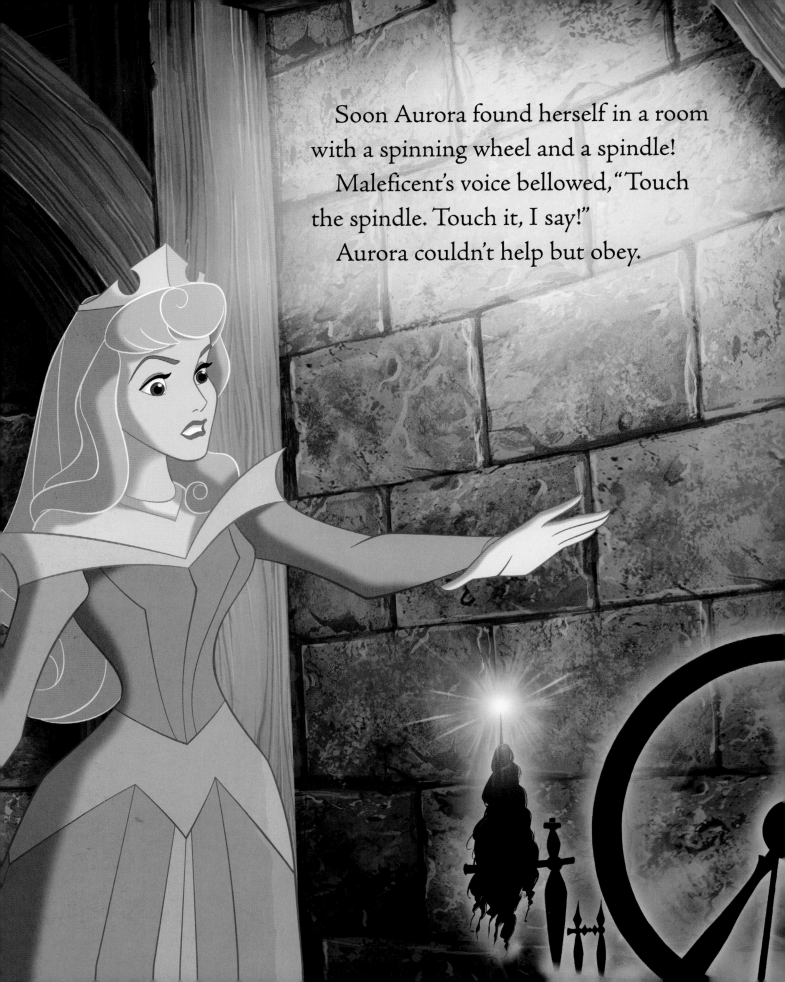

Soon Aurora found herself in a room
with a spinning wheel and a spindle!
Maleficent's voice bellowed, "Touch
the spindle. Touch it, I say!"
Aurora couldn't help but obey.

When the fairies finally reached the hidden room, they saw Maleficent standing in triumph beside the fallen princess. "You poor simple *fools*," Maleficent cried. "Thinking you could defeat me, *me*, the mistress of all evil!" Then, with a wicked laugh, she disappeared.

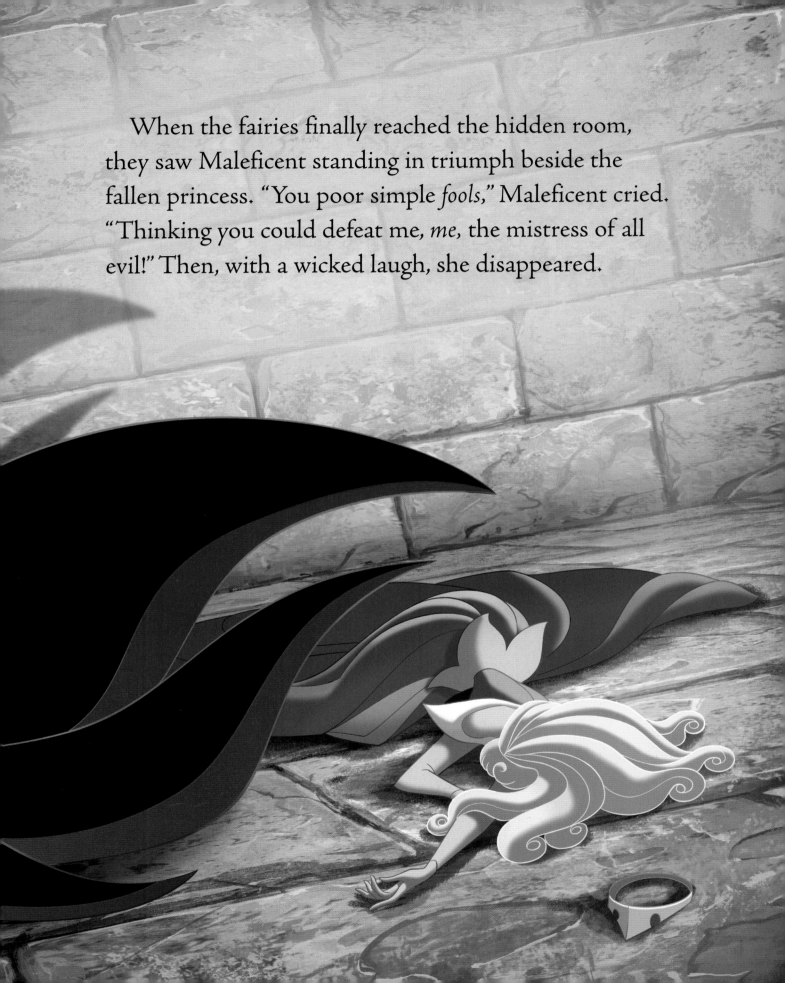

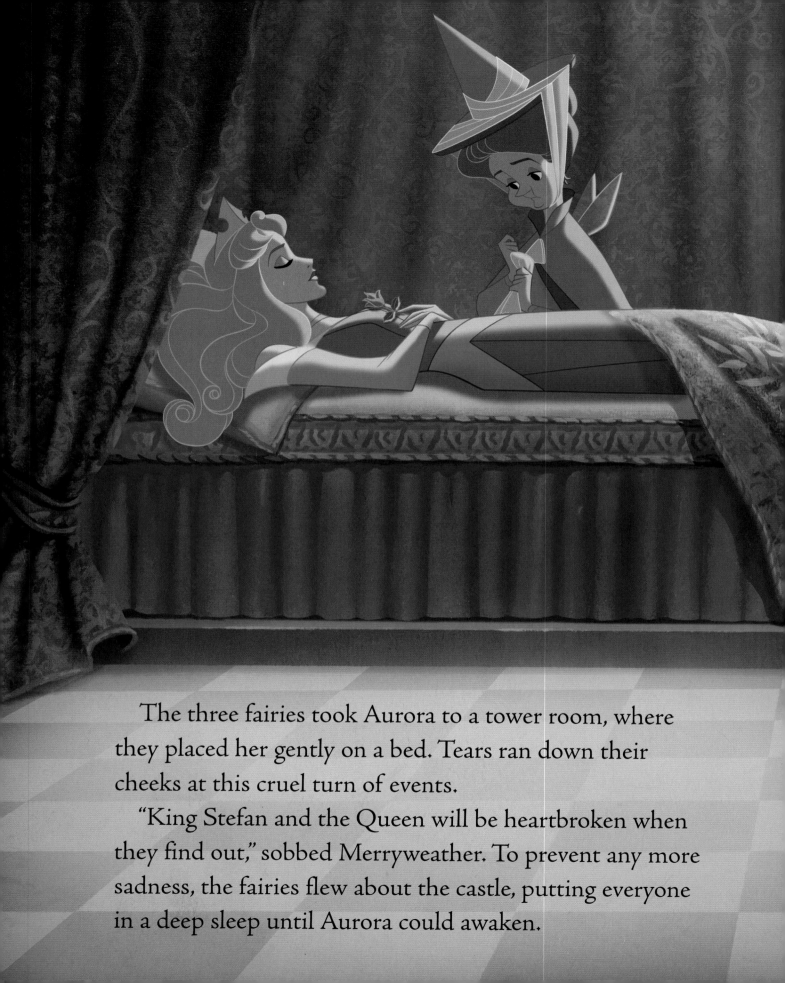

The three fairies took Aurora to a tower room, where
they placed her gently on a bed. Tears ran down their
cheeks at this cruel turn of events.

"King Stefan and the Queen will be heartbroken when
they find out," sobbed Merryweather. To prevent any more
sadness, the fairies flew about the castle, putting everyone
in a deep sleep until Aurora could awaken.

Not long after, Phillip arrived at the cottage,
expecting to see the lovely girl from the forest. Instead,
Maleficent and her henchmen were waiting. The evil
fairy wanted to ensure that Briar Rose's young prince
would not save her.

After locking Prince Phillip in her dungeon,
Maleficent revealed that the girl he had fallen in love
with was Princess Aurora—and that she was under a
spell that only True Love's Kiss could break.

When wicked Maleficent finally left, the good fairies came to the rescue. They released Phillip from his chains and armed him with the enchanted Shield of Virtue and the mighty Sword of Truth.

With help from the fairies, Phillip fought his way past Maleficent's henchmen and through a wall of thorny bushes.

Suddenly, Maleficent turned herself into an enormous fire-breathing dragon! Phillip bravely used his shield to protect himself from the heat and force of the flames.

Teetering at the edge of a cliff, Phillip took aim and threw his sword, striking Maleficent in the chest. She stumbled and fell. The evil fairy was defeated.

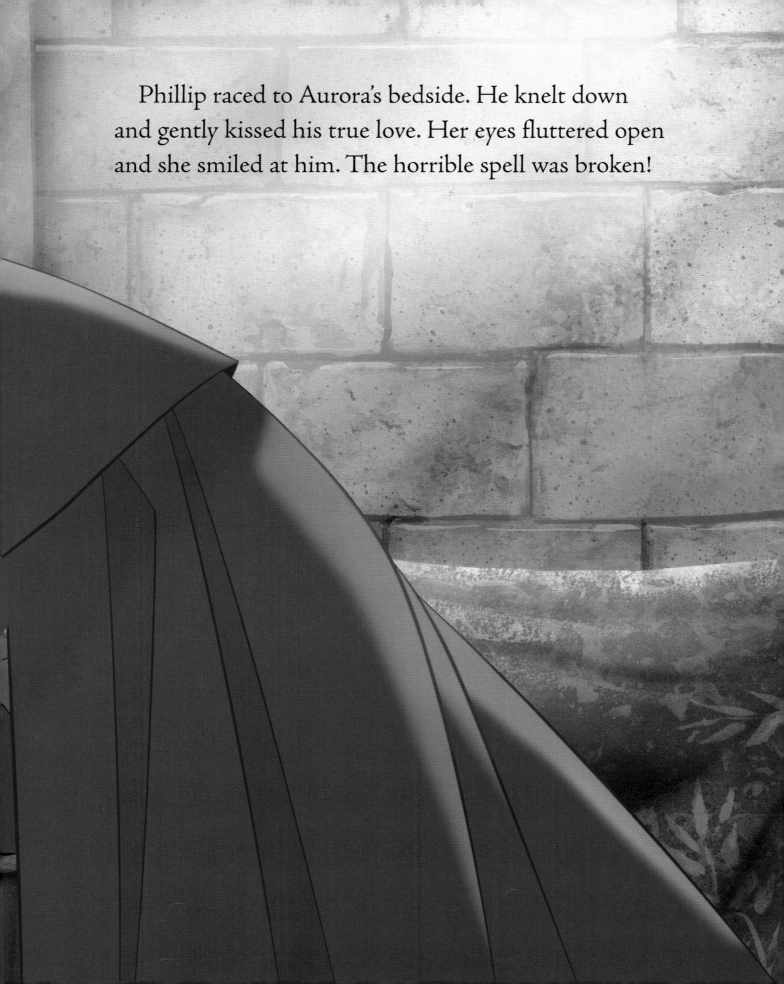

Phillip raced to Aurora's bedside. He knelt down
and gently kissed his true love. Her eyes fluttered open
and she smiled at him. The horrible spell was broken!

The good fairies quickly woke up everyone in the castle. King Hubert, King Stefan, and the Queen yawned and stretched, but no one realized that they had all been asleep.

Phillip and Aurora entered the room and bowed
before the throne. Then Aurora rushed into the arms of
her parents and felt their warm embrace for the first time
in sixteen years.

Prince Phillip took Princess Aurora's hand. Then, just as they had when they first met, the happy couple began to dance. And the entire kingdom rejoiced.